Milly-Molly-Mandy Stories

Joyce Lankester Brisley wrote and drew books from an early age; she had her first fairy story published in a children's paper at the age of thirteen. She studied at art school and, when she was twenty, had pictures hung in the Royal Academy. However, she enjoyed writing and illustrating stories best, and her immortal creation, the Milly-Molly-Mandy series, set a seal on her success. Miss Brisley died in 1978 aged eighty-two.

Joyce Lankester Brisley

Milly-Molly-Mandy Stories

Stories

PUFFIN

PUFFIN BOOKS

Published by the Penguin Group
Penguin Books Ltd, 80 Strand, London WC2R 0RL, England
Penguin Group (USA) Inc., 375 Hudson Street, New York, New York 10014, USA
Penguin Group (Canada), 90 Eglinton Avenue East, Suite 700, Toronto, Ontario, Canada M4P 2Y3
(a division of Pearson Penguin Canada Inc.)
Penguin Ireland, 25 St Stephen's Green, Dublin 2, Ireland (a division of Penguin Books Ltd)
Penguin Group (Australia), 250 Camberwell Road, Camberwell, Victoria 3124, Australia
(a division of Pearson Australia Group Pty Ltd)
Penguin Books India Pvt Ltd, 11 Community Centre, Panchsheel Park,
New Delhi – 110 017, India
Penguin Group (NZ), 67 Apollo Drive, Rosedale, North Shore 0632, New Zealand
(a division of Pearson New Zealand Ltd)
Penguin Books (South Africa) (Pty) Ltd, 24 Sturdee Avenue, Rosebank,
Johannesburg 2196, South Africa

Penguin Books Ltd, Registered Offices: 80 Strand, London WC2R 0RL, England

puffinbooks.com

First published by Harrap 1928
Published in Puffin Books 1972
Published in this edition 2007
This edition produced for The Book People Ltd,
Hall Wood Avenue, Haydock, St Helens, WA11 9UL
1

Text copyright © Joyce Lankester Brisley, 1928
Introduction copyright © Julia Eccleshare, 2007
All rights reserved

The moral right of the author has been asserted

Set in 15/22 pt Perpetua
Typeset by Palimpsest Book Production Limited, Grangemouth, Stirlingshire
Made and printed in England by Clays Ltd, St Ives plc

British Library Cataloguing in Publication Data
A CIP catalogue record for this book is available from the British Library

ISBN: 978-0-141-33702-9

www.greenpenguin.co.uk

INTRODUCTION

BY JULIA ECCLESHARE, SERIES EDITOR

Milly-Molly-Mandy lived a long, long time ago in
another kind of childhood altogether. She can wander
to the village shop alone; walk to school alone; speak
to anyone she likes and do many other things which
are now outside the experience of children today. She
doesn't travel far; she doesn't have to. What she needs
is near at hand. She already lives with her parents,
grandparents and her aunt and uncle who provide
quite enough company. And yet how Milly-Molly-
Mandy behaves, her little triumphs as she becomes
more independent, her love of animals, and, above all,
the importance of her friendship with her 'little-friend-
Susan' and especially her delight when Susan comes
to stay are instantly recognizable to children anywhere
and at any time. A bit of a goody-goody – well, it
would be hard not to be with a name like Milly-
Molly-Mandy – she's just a little girl having some
hugely satisfying if simple adventures.

As a child who could never have managed to be as
good as Milly-Molly-Mandy I used to think of her as
a little bit soppy but, on re-reading these stories, it is

easy to see that though Milly-Molly-Mandy is no rebel she is nonetheless sparky and independent-minded, as in 'Milly-Molly-Mandy Goes Errands' when she makes her own decision about how to spend her money, which is clever and canny.

When *Milly-Molly-Mandy Stories* was first published, the little girl at the heart of them represented the daily ups and downs of a not untypical, country childhood. For today's reader, in addition to the joy of sharing Milly-Molly-Mandy's delight at her life, there is the added curiosity and undoubted pleasure of seeing how different childhood once was.

Contents

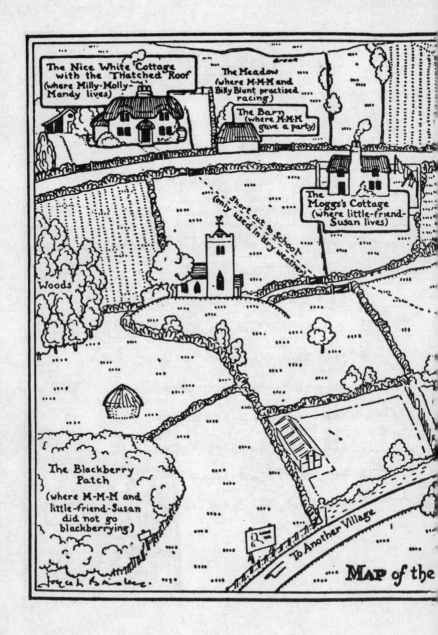

The Nice White Cottage
with the Thatched Roof
(where Milly-Molly-
Mandy lives)

The Meadow
(where M-M-M and
Billy Blunt practised
racing)

The Barn
(where M·M·M
gave a party)

The Moggs's Cottage
(where little-friend-
Susan lives)

Brook

Short cut to School
(only used in dry weather)

Woods

The Blackberry
Patch

(where M-M-M and
little-friend-Susan
did not go
blackberrying)

To Another Village

MAP of the

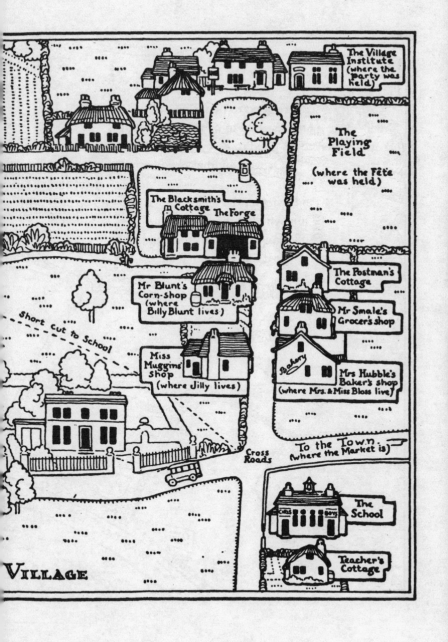

The Village Institute (where the party was held)

The Playing Field (where the Fête was held)

The Blacksmith's Cottage The Forge

The Postman's Cottage

Mr Blunt's Corn-shop (where Billy Blunt lives)

Mr Smale's Grocer's shop

Short cut to School

Miss Muggins' Shop (where Jilly lives)

Bakery

Mrs Hubble's Baker's shop (where Mrs & Miss Bloss live)

To the Town (where the Market is)

Cross Roads

The School

GIRLS BOYS

Teacher's Cottage

VILLAGE

It's good to be sitting still,
And it's good to be running wild,
And it's good to be by yourself alone
Or with another child.

And whether the child's grown up,
Or whether the child is small,
So long as it really is a Child
It doesn't matter at all.

J. L. B.

Chapter One

Milly-Molly-Mandy Goes Errands

Once upon a time there was a little girl.

She had a Father, and a Mother, and a
Grandpa, and a Grandma, and an Uncle, and
an Aunty; and they all lived together in a nice
white cottage with a thatched roof.

This little girl had short hair, and short legs,
and short frocks (pink-and-white-striped cotton
in summer, and red serge in winter). But her
name wasn't short at all. It was Millicent
Margaret Amanda. But Father and Mother and
Grandpa and Grandma and Uncle and Aunty
couldn't very well call out 'Millicent Margaret
Amanda!' every time they wanted her, so they

shortened it to 'Milly-Molly-Mandy', which is quite easy to say.

Now everybody in the nice white cottage with the thatched roof had some particular job to do – even Milly-Molly-Mandy.

Father grew vegetables in the big garden by the cottage. Mother cooked the dinners and did the washing. Grandpa took the vegetables to market in his little pony-cart. Grandma knitted socks and mittens and nice warm woollies for them all. Uncle kept cows (to give them milk) and chickens (to give them eggs). Aunty sewed frocks and shirts for them, and did the sweeping and dusting.

And Milly-Molly-Mandy, what did she do?

Well, Milly-Molly-Mandy's legs were short, as I've told you, but they were very lively, just right for running errands. So

Milly-Molly-Mandy was quite busy, fetching
and carrying things, and taking messages.

One fine day Milly-Molly-Mandy was in the
garden playing with Toby the dog, when Father
poked his head out from the other side of a big
row of beans, and said:

'Milly-Molly-Mandy, run down to Mr
Moggs's cottage and ask for the trowel he
borrowed of me!'

So Milly-Molly-Mandy said 'Yes, Farver!' and
ran in to get her hat.

3

At the kitchen door was Mother, with a basket of eggs in her hand. And when she saw Milly-Molly-Mandy she said:

'Milly-Molly-Mandy, run down to Mrs Moggs and give her these eggs. She's got visitors.'

So Milly-Molly-Mandy said 'Yes, Muvver!' and took the basket. 'Trowel for Farver, eggs for Muvver,' she thought to herself.

Then Grandpa came up and said:

'Milly-Molly-Mandy, please get me a ball of string from Miss Muggins's shop – here's the penny.'

So Milly-Molly-Mandy said 'Yes, Grandpa!' and took the penny, thinking to herself, 'Trowel for Farver, eggs for Muvver, string for Grandpa.'

As she passed through the kitchen Grandma, who was sitting in her armchair knitting, said:

'Milly-Molly-Mandy, will you get me a skein of red wool? Here's a sixpence.'

So Milly-Molly-Mandy said 'Yes, Grandma!' and took the sixpence. 'Trowel for Farver, eggs for Muvver, string for Grandpa, red wool for Grandma,' she whispered over to herself.

As she went into the passage Uncle came striding up in a hurry.

'Oh, Milly-Molly-Mandy,' said Uncle, 'run like a good girl to Mr Blunt's shop, and tell him I'm waiting for the chicken-feed he promised to send!'

So Milly-Molly-Mandy said 'Yes, Uncle!' and thought to herself, 'Trowel for Farver, eggs for Muvver, string for Grandpa, red wool for Grandma, chicken-feed for Uncle.'

As she got her hat off the peg Aunty called from the parlour where she was dusting:

'Is that Milly-Molly-Mandy? Will you get

me a packet of needles, dear? Here's a penny!'

So Milly-Molly-Mandy said 'Yes, Aunty!' and took the penny, thinking to herself, 'Trowel for Farver, eggs for Muvver, string for Grandpa, red wool for Grandma, chicken-feed for Uncle, needles for Aunty, and I do hope there won't be anything more!'

But there was nothing else, so Milly-Molly-Mandy started out down the path. When she came to the gate Toby the dog capered up, looking very excited at the thought of a walk. But Milly-Molly-Mandy eyed him solemnly, and said:

'Trowel for Farver, eggs for Muvver, string for Grandpa, red wool for Grandma, chicken-feed for Uncle, needles for Aunty. No, Toby, you mustn't come now, I've too much to think about. But I promise to take you for a walk when I come back!'

GRANDPA · GRANDMA · FATHER · MOTHER · UNCLE · AUNTY · MILLY-MOLLY-MANDY.

So she left Toby on the other side of the gate, and set off down the road, with the basket and the pennies and the sixpence.

Presently she met a little friend, and the little friend said:

'Hello, Milly-Molly-Mandy! I've got a new see-saw! Do come on it with me!'

But Milly-Molly-Mandy looked at her solemnly and said:

'Trowel for Farver, eggs for Muvver, string for Grandpa, red wool for Grandma, chicken-feed for Uncle, needles for Aunty. No, Susan, I can't come now, I'm busy. But I'd like to come when I get back – after I've taken Toby for a walk.'

So Milly-Molly-Mandy went on her way with the basket and the pennies and the sixpence.

Soon she came to the Moggs's cottage.

'Please, Mrs Moggs, can I have the trowel

for Farver? – and here are some eggs from
Muvver!' she said.

Mrs Moggs was very much obliged indeed
for the eggs, and fetched the trowel and a
piece of seed-cake for Milly-Molly-Mandy's
own self. And Milly-Molly-Mandy went on her
way with the empty basket.

Next she came to Miss Muggins's little shop.

'Please, Miss Muggins, can I have a ball of
string for Grandpa and a skein of red wool for
Grandma?'

So Miss Muggins put the string and the wool
into Milly-Molly-Mandy's basket, and took a
penny and a sixpence in exchange. So that left
Milly-Molly-Mandy with one penny. And Milly-
Molly-Mandy couldn't remember what that
penny was for.

'Sweeties, perhaps?' said Miss Muggins,
glancing at the row of glass bottles on the shelf.

But Milly-Molly-Mandy shook her head.

'No,' she said, 'and it can't be chicken-feed for Uncle, because that would be more than a penny, only I haven't got to pay for it.'

'It must be sweeties!' said Miss Muggins.

'No,' said Milly-Molly-Mandy, 'but I'll remember soon. Good morning, Miss Muggins!'

So Milly-Molly-Mandy went on to Mr Blunt's, and gave him Uncle's message, and then she sat down on the doorstep and thought what that penny could be for.

And she couldn't remember.

But she remembered one thing: 'It's for Aunty,' she thought, 'and I love Aunty.' And she thought for just a little while longer. Then suddenly she sprang up and went back to Miss Muggins's shop.

'I've remembered!' she said. 'It's needles for Aunty!'

So Miss Muggins put the packet of needles
into the basket, and took the penny, and Milly-
Molly-Mandy set off for home.

'That's a good little messenger to remember
all those things!' said Mother, when she got
there. They were just going to begin dinner. 'I
thought you were only going with my eggs!'

'She went for my trowel!' said Father.

'And my string!' said Grandpa.

'And my wool!' said Grandma.

'And my chicken-feed!' said Uncle.

'And my needles!' said Aunty.

Then they all laughed; and Grandpa, feeling in his pocket, said:

'Well, here's another errand for you – go and get yourself some sweeties!'

So after dinner Toby had a nice walk and his mistress got her sweets. And then Milly-Molly-Mandy and little-friend-Susan had a lovely time on the see-saw, chatting and eating raspberry-drops, and feeling very happy and contented indeed.

Chapter Two

Milly-Molly-Mandy Spends a Penny

Once upon a time Milly-Molly-Mandy found a penny in the pocket of an old coat.

Milly-Molly-Mandy felt very rich indeed.

She thought of all the things she could buy with it, and there were so many that she did not know which to choose. (That is the worst of a penny.) So Milly-Molly-Mandy asked everybody with whom she lived, in the nice white cottage with the thatched roof, what they would do with it if they were her.

'Put it in the bank,' said Grandpa promptly. He was making up accounts. Milly-Molly-Mandy thought that a wise idea.

'Buy a skein of rainbow wool and learn to knit,' said Grandma, who was knitting by the kitchen door. Milly-Molly-Mandy thought that a good idea.

'Buy some seeds and grow mustard-and-cress,' said Father, who was gardening. Milly-Molly-Mandy thought that quite a good idea.

'Buy a little patty-pan and make a cake in it,' said Mother, who was cooking. Milly-Molly-Mandy thought that a very good idea.

'Save it up until you get three, and I'll let you buy a baby duckling with them,' said Uncle, who was scooping out corn for his chickens. Milly-Molly-Mandy thought that an excellent idea.

'Get some sweets,' said Aunty, who was very busy sewing, and did not want to be interrupted. Milly-Molly-Mandy thought that a very pleasant idea.

Then she went to her own little corner of the garden for a 'think', for she still could not make up her mind which of all those nice things to do. She thought and thought for a long time.

And then – what do you think she bought?

Some mustard-and-cress seeds, which she planted in a shallow box of earth and stood in a nice warm place by the tool-shed.

She watered it every day, and shaded it if the sun were too hot; and at last the little seeds grew into a lovely clump of fresh green mustard-and-cress, that made you quite long for some bread-and-butter to eat it with.

When it was ready to cut Milly-Molly-Mandy went to Mrs Moggs, their neighbour down the road, who sometimes had summer visitors.

'Mrs Moggs,' said Milly-Molly-Mandy, 'if you should want some mustard-and-cress for your visitors' tea I have some to sell. It's very good, and quite cheap.'

'Why Milly-Molly-Mandy,' said Mrs Moggs, 'that's exactly what I am wanting! Is it ready for cutting now?'

So Milly-Molly-Mandy ran home and borrowed a pair of scissors and a little basket, and she snipped that lovely clump of fresh green mustard-and-cress (all but a tiny bit for her own tea) and carried it to Mrs Moggs.

And Mrs Moggs gave her twopence for it.

So Milly-Molly-Mandy had done one of the

nice things and spent her penny, and now she had twopence!

Then Milly-Molly-Mandy took one of the pennies to the little village shop, and bought a skein of beautiful rainbow wool.

'Grandma,' she said, when she got home, 'please will you teach me to knit a kettle-holder?'

So Grandma found some knitting-needles and showed Milly-Molly-Mandy how to knit. And though it had to be undone several times at first, Milly-Molly-Mandy really did knit quite a nice kettle-holder, and there was just enough wool for it.

When she had put a loop in one corner to hang it up by she went to Mother, who was just putting the potatoes on to boil.

'Mother,' said Milly-Molly-Mandy, 'would you think this kettle-holder worth a penny?'

'Why, Milly-Molly-Mandy,' said Mother, 'that is exactly what I am wanting, for my old one is all worn out! But the penny only pays for the wool, so you are making me a present of all your trouble.' And Mother gave Milly-Molly-Mandy a penny and a kiss, and Milly-Molly-Mandy felt well paid.

So Milly-Molly-Mandy had done another of the nice things, had spent her penny, and learnt to knit, and still she had her penny!

Then Milly-Molly-Mandy took her penny down to the little village shop and bought a shiny tin patty-pan. And next baking-day Mother let her make a little cake in the patty-pan and put it in the oven. And it was such a beautiful little cake, and so nicely browned, that it seemed almost too good to eat.

Milly-Molly-Mandy put it outside on the window-sill to cool.

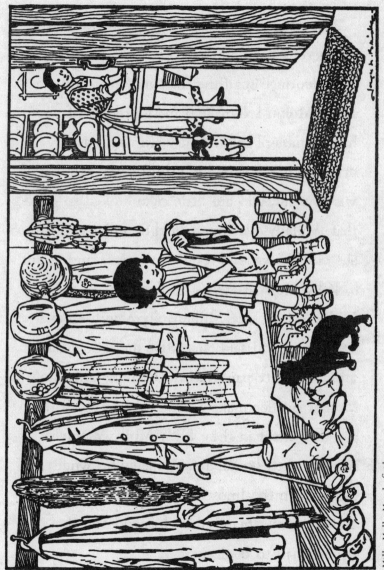

Milly-Molly-Mandy finds a penny

Presently along came a lady cyclist, and as it was a very hot day she stopped at the nice white cottage with the thatched roof, and asked Milly-Molly-Mandy's Mother if she could have a glass of milk. And while she was drinking it she saw the little cake on the window-sill, and the little cake looked so good that the lady cyclist felt hungry and asked if she could have that too.

Milly-Molly-Mandy's Mother looked at Milly-Molly-Mandy, and Milly-Molly-Mandy gave a little gulp, and said 'Yes.' And the lady cyclist ate up the little patty-cake. And she did enjoy it!

When she had gone Milly-Molly-Mandy's Mother took up the pennies the lady cyclist had put on the table for the milk and the cake, and she gave one to Milly-Molly-Mandy because it was her cake.

So Milly-Molly-Mandy had done yet another of the nice things and spent her penny, but still she had her penny.

Then Milly-Molly-Mandy took her penny down to the little village shop and bought some sweets, lovely big aniseed-balls, that changed colour as you sucked them.

She would not eat one until she got home, and then gave one to Grandpa and one to Grandma and one to Father and one to Mother and one to Uncle and one to Aunty. And then she found there were six for herself, so she ate them, and they were very nice.

So Milly-Molly-Mandy had done another of the nice things and spent her penny. But she still had one penny from the mustard-and-cress.

Then she went to Grandpa, and asked him please to put it in the bank for her.

And then she went to Uncle.

'Uncle,' said Milly-Molly-Mandy, 'I've done everything with my penny that everybody said, but you. And though I can't buy a little baby duckling yet, I've got a penny saved towards it, in the bank.'

And it was not very long before Milly-Molly-Mandy had saved up to threepence; and then Uncle let her have a little yellow baby duckling all for her own.

Chapter Three

Milly-Molly-Mandy Meets her Great-Aunt

Once upon a time, one fine evening, Milly-Molly-Mandy and her Father and Mother and Grandpa and Grandma and Uncle and Aunty were all sitting at supper (there was bread-and-butter and cheese for the grown-ups, and bread-and-milk for Milly-Molly-Mandy, and baked apples and cocoa for them all), when suddenly there came a loud *Bang-bang!* on the knocker.

'Run, Milly-Molly-Mandy,' said Mother. 'That sounds like the postman!'

So Milly-Molly-Mandy jumped down from her chair in a great hurry, and fetched the

letter, which was for Mother. Then she climbed
on her chair again, and everyone looked
interested while Mother opened it.

It was from someone who called Milly-
Molly-Mandy's Mother 'Dear Polly', and was
to ask if that someone might spend a few days
with them, and it finished up, 'Your
affectionate Aunt Margaret'.

Father and Mother and Grandpa and
Grandma and Uncle and Aunty were quite
pleased, and Milly-Molly-Mandy was pleased
too, although she did not know who it was
until Grandma said to her, 'It is my sister

Margaret, your great-aunty, who is coming.'
Then Milly-Molly-Mandy was very interested
indeed.

'Is she my great-aunty and your sister too?'
she asked Grandma.

'Yes, and she's my sister-in-law,' said
Grandpa.

'And my aunty,' said Mother.

'And my aunty-in-law,' said Father.

'And my aunty-in-law too,' said Aunty.

'And my aunty,' said Uncle.

'Fancy!' said Milly-Molly-Mandy. 'She's all
that, and she's a great-aunty too! I would like
to see her!'

The next day Milly-Molly-Mandy helped
Mother make up the spare-room bed.

'I could wish the spare room were a little
bigger,' said Mother, and Milly-Molly-Mandy
looked around gravely, and thought it really

'That sounds like the postman!'

was rather small for a great-aunty. But she went and fetched some marigolds from her own little garden, and put them in a vase on the chest of drawers, for she knew there was lots of room for love, even if there was not much for great-aunties.

Then Milly-Molly-Mandy helped Father bring the big armchair out of the best parlour into the room where they always sat. Milly-Molly-Mandy was glad it was such a big chair – it really looked quite large enough even for a great-aunty.

Then Mother cooked some big fruit-cakes and some little seed-cakes and some sponge-cakes and a whole lot of other things, and Milly-Molly-Mandy (who helped to clean up the cooking-bowls and spoons) supposed a great-aunty must take quite a lot of feeding.

As soon as ever the last bowl was scraped

Milly-Molly-Mandy ran down the road to tell little-friend-Susan the news.

Little-friend-Susan was walking on the wall, but she jumped down as soon as she saw Milly-Molly-Mandy.

'Oh, Susan!' said Milly-Molly-Mandy, 'you know my Aunty?'

'Yes,' said little-friend-Susan.

'Well,' said Milly-Molly-Mandy, 'she's just a usual aunty, but I've got a great-aunty coming to stay with us!'

Little-friend-Susan, being a best friend, was just as interested as Milly-Molly-Mandy, and it was soon settled that next morning she should come and play in Milly-Molly-Mandy's garden, so that she might see Great-Aunty Margaret for herself.

Then Milly-Molly-Mandy ran back home to dinner.

After dinner Mother and Grandma and Aunty and Milly-Molly-Mandy hurried through the washing-up, and tidied the cottage, while Father put the pony in the trap. And then they changed their dresses, while Father drove to the station.

And then Milly-Molly-Mandy, in her clean frock, kept running to the gate to see if the pony-trap were in sight yet.

And at last it was – and Milly-Molly-Mandy was so excited that she raced into the cottage and jumped up and down, and then she ran out to the gate again, and opened it wide.

The pony trotted up to the gate and stopped, and Father got down first. And then he took down Great-Aunty Margaret's great basket. And then he helped down Great-Aunty Margaret her own self!

And what do you think Great-Aunty
Margaret was like?

She was a little, little, white-haired lady, in a
black bonnet and dress spotted with little
mauve flowers, and she had a kind little face
with pink cheeks.

Milly-Molly-Mandy was so surprised, it was
all she could do to mind her manners and not
stare.

Great-Aunty Margaret was soon seated in the
great armchair, and instead of filling it, as
Milly-Molly-Mandy had expected, why – there
was heaps of room for Milly-Molly-Mandy

there too! And instead of eating up all the big
fruit-cakes and the little seed-cakes and the
sponge-cakes and other things, there was lots
for everybody in the family, including Milly-
Molly-Mandy.

And as for the spare room being too small, it
looked almost big, because Great-Aunty
Margaret was such a little lady.

When Great-Aunty Margaret saw the flowers
on her chest of drawers she said gently:

'Why, Millicent Margaret Amanda, I believe
that is your doing! Thank you, my dearie!'

'Oh, Great-Aunty Margaret!' said Milly-
Molly-Mandy, reaching to kiss her again. 'I do
like you! Would you mind if I showed you to
Susan this evening, instead of making her wait
till tomorrow?'

Chapter Four

Milly-Molly-Mandy Goes Blackberrying

Once upon a time Milly-Molly-Mandy found some big ripe blackberries on her way home from school. There were six great beauties and one little hard one, so Milly-Molly-Mandy put the little hard one in her mouth and carried the others home on a leaf.

She gave one to Father, and Father said, 'Ah! that makes me think the time for blackberry puddings has come!'

Then she gave one to Mother, and asked what it made her think of. And Mother said, 'A whole row of pots of blackberry jam that I ought to have in my store-board!'

Then she gave one to Grandpa, and Grandpa
said it made him think 'Blackberry tart!'

And Grandma said, 'Blackberry jelly!'

And Uncle said, 'Stewed blackberry-and-
apple!'

And Aunty said, 'A plate of fresh blackberries
with sugar and cream!'

'My!' thought Milly-Molly-Mandy, as she
threw away the empty leaf, 'I must get a big,
big basket and go blackberrying the very next
Saturday, so that there can be lots of puddings
and jam and tarts and jelly and stewed
blackberry-and-apple and fresh blackberries,
for Farver and Muvver and Grandpa and

Grandma and Uncle and Aunty – and me! I'll ask Susan to come too.'

So the very next Saturday Milly-Molly-Mandy and little-friend-Susan set out with big baskets (to hold the blackberries) and hooked sticks (to pull the brambles nearer) and stout boots (to keep the prickles off) and old frocks (lest the thorns should catch). And they walked and they walked, till they came to a place where they knew there was always a lot of blackberries – at the proper time of year, of course.

But when they came to the place – oh, dear! – they saw a notice-board stuck up just inside a gap in the fence. And the notice-board said, as plain as anything:

TRESPASSERS

WILL BE

PROSECUTED

Milly-Molly-Mandy and little-friend-Susan knew that meant 'You mustn't come here, because the owner doesn't want you, and it's his land.'

Milly-Molly-Mandy and little-friend-Susan looked at each other very solemnly indeed. Then Milly-Molly-Mandy said, 'I don't s'pose anyone would see if we went in.'

And little-friend-Susan said, 'I don't s'pose they'd miss any of the blackberries.'

And Milly-Molly-Mandy said, 'But it wouldn't be right.'

And little-friend-Susan shook her head very firmly.

So they took up their baskets and sticks and moved away, trying not to feel hurt about it, although they had come a long way to that place.

They didn't know quite what to do with

themselves after that, for there seemed to be no blackberries anywhere else, so they amused themselves by walking in a dry ditch close by the fence, shuffling along in the leaves with their stout little boots that were to have kept the prickles off.

And suddenly – what do you think they saw? A little ball of brown fur, just ahead of them among the grasses in the ditch.

'Is it a rabbit?' whispered little-friend-Susan. They crept closer.

'It is a rabbit!' whispered Milly-Molly-Mandy.

'Why doesn't it run away?' said little-friend-Susan, and she stroked it. The little ball of fur wriggled. Then Milly-Molly-Mandy stroked it, and it wriggled again.

Then Milly-Molly-Mandy exclaimed, 'I believe it's got its head stuck in a hole in the bank!'

Milly-Molly-Mandy and little-friend-Susan set out

And they looked, and that was just what had happened. Some earth had fallen down as bunny was burrowing, and it couldn't get its head out again.

So Milly-Molly-Mandy and little-friend-Susan carefully dug with their fingers, and loosened the earth round about, and as soon as bunny's head was free he shook his ears and stared at them.

Milly-Molly-Mandy and little-friend-Susan sat very still, and only smiled and nodded gently to show him he needn't be afraid, because they loved him.

And then little bunny turned his head and ran skitter-scutter along the ditch and up the bank, into the wood and was gone.

'Oh!' said Milly-Molly-Mandy, 'we always wanted a rabbit, and now we've got one, Susan!'

'Only we'd rather ours played in the fields with his brothers and sisters instead of stopping in a poky hutch,' said little-friend-Susan.

'And if we'd gone trespassing we should never have come here and found him,' said Milly-Molly-Mandy. 'I'd much rather have a little rabbit than a whole lot of blackberries.'

And when they got back to the nice white cottage with the thatched roof, where Milly-Molly-Mandy lived, Father and Mother and Grandpa and Grandma and Uncle and Aunty all said they would much rather have a little rabbit running about in the woods than all the finest blackberries in the world.

However, the next Saturday Milly-Molly-Mandy and little-friend-Susan came upon a splendid place for blackberrying, without any notice-board; and Milly-Molly-Mandy gathered such a big basketful that there was enough to make blackberry puddings and jam and tarts and jelly and stewed blackberry-and-apple and fresh blackberries for Father and Mother and Grandpa and Grandma and Uncle and Aunty – and Milly-Molly-Mandy too.

And all the time a little rabbit skipped about in the woods and thought what a lovely world it was.

(And that's a true story!)

Chapter Five

Milly-Molly-Mandy Goes to a Party

Once upon a time something very nice happened in the village where Milly-Molly-Mandy and her Father and Mother and Grandpa and Grandma and Uncle and Aunty lived. Some ladies clubbed together to give a party to all the children in the village, and of course Milly-Molly-Mandy was invited.

Little-friend-Susan had an invitation too, and Billy Blunt (whose father kept the corn-shop where Milly-Molly-Mandy's Uncle got his chicken-feed), and Jilly, the little niece of Miss Muggins (who kept the shop where Milly-Molly-Mandy's Grandma bought her knitting-wool), and lots of others whom Milly-Molly-Mandy knew.

It was exciting.

Milly-Molly-Mandy had not been to a real party for a long time, so she was very pleased and interested when Mother said, 'Well, Milly-Molly-Mandy, you must have a proper new dress for a party like this. We must think what we can do.'

So Mother and Grandma and Aunty thought together for a bit, and then Mother went to the big wardrobe and rummaged in her bottom drawer until she found a most beautiful white silk scarf, which she had worn when she was married to Father, and it was just wide enough to be made into a party frock for Milly-Molly-Mandy.

Then Grandma brought out of her best handkerchief-box a most beautiful lace handkerchief, which would just cut into a little collar for the neck of the party frock.

And Aunty brought out of her small top drawer some most beautiful pink ribbon, all smelling of lavender – just enough to make into a sash for the party frock.

And then Mother and Aunty set to work to cut and stitch at the party frock, while Milly-Molly-Mandy jumped up and down and handed pins when they were wanted.

The next day Father came in with a paper parcel for Milly-Molly-Mandy bulging in his coat-pocket, and when Milly-Molly-Mandy unwrapped it she found the most beautiful little pair of red shoes inside!

And then Grandpa came in and held out his closed hand to Milly-Molly-Mandy, and when Milly-Molly-Mandy got his fingers open she found the most beautiful little coral necklace inside!

And then Uncle came in, and he said to Milly-Molly-Mandy, 'What have I done with my handkerchief?' And he felt in all his pockets. 'Oh, here it is!' And he pulled out the most beautiful little handkerchief with a pink border, which of course Milly-Molly-Mandy just knew was meant for her, and she wouldn't let Uncle wipe his nose on it, which he pretended he was going to do!

Milly-Molly-Mandy was so pleased she hugged everybody in turn – Father, Mother,

Grandpa, Grandma, Uncle, and Aunty.

At last the great day arrived, and little-friend-Susan, in her best spotted dress and silver bangle, called for Milly-Molly-Mandy, and they went together to the village institute, where the party was to be.

There was a lady outside who welcomed them in, and there were more ladies inside who helped them to take their things off. And everywhere looked so pretty, with garlands of coloured paper looped from the ceiling, and everybody in their best clothes.

Most of the boys and girls were looking at a row of toys on the mantelpiece, and a lady explained that they were all prizes, to be won by the children who got the most marks in the games they were going to have. There was a lovely fairy doll and a big Teddy Bear and a picture-book and all sorts of things.

And at the end of the row was a funny little white cotton-wool rabbit with a pointed paper hat on his head. And directly Milly-Molly-Mandy saw him she wanted him dreadfully badly, more than any of the other things.

Little-friend-Susan wanted the picture-book, and Miss Muggins's niece, Jilly, wanted the fairy doll. But the black, beady eyes of the little cotton-wool rabbit gazed so wistfully at Milly-Molly-Mandy that she determined to try ever so hard in all the games and see if she could win him.

Then the games began, and they were fun! They had a spoon-and-potato race, and musical chairs, and putting the tail on the donkey blindfold, and all sorts of guessing-games.

And then they had supper – bread-and-butter with coloured hundreds-and-thousands sprinkled on, and red jellies and yellow jellies,

At last the great day arrived

and cakes with icing and cakes with cherries, and lemonade in red glasses.

It was quite a proper party.

And at the end the names of prize-winners were called out, and the children had to go up and receive their prizes.

And what do you think Milly-Molly-Mandy got?

Why, she had tried so hard to win the little cotton-wool rabbit that she won first prize instead, and got the lovely fairy doll!

And Miss Muggins's niece Jilly, who hadn't won any of the games, got the little cotton-wool rabbit with the sad, beady eyes – for do you know, the cotton-wool rabbit was only the booby prize, after all!

It was a lovely fairy doll, but Milly-Molly-Mandy was sure Miss Muggins's Jilly wasn't loving the booby rabbit as it ought to be loved,

for its beady eyes did look so sad, and when
she got near Miss Muggins's Jilly she stroked
the booby rabbit, and Miss Muggins's Jilly
stroked the fairy doll's hair.

Then Milly-Molly-Mandy said, 'Do you love
the fairy doll more than the booby rabbit?'

And Miss Muggins's Jilly said, 'I should think
so!'

So Milly-Molly-Mandy ran up to the lady
who had given the prizes, and asked if she and
Miss Muggins's Jilly might exchange prizes,
and the lady said, 'Yes, of course.'

So Milly-Molly-Mandy and the booby rabbit

went home together to the nice white cottage with the thatched roof, and Father and Mother and Grandpa and Grandma and Uncle and Aunty all liked the booby rabbit very much indeed.

And do you know, one day one of his little bead eyes dropped off, and when Mother had stuck it on again with a dab of glue, his eyes didn't look a bit sad any more, but almost as happy as Milly-Molly-Mandy's own!

Chapter Six

Milly-Molly-Mandy Enjoys a Visit

Once upon a time Milly-Molly-Mandy was
invited to go for a little visit to an old friend
of Mother's who lived in a nearby town.
Uncle was to take her in the pony-trap on
Saturday morning on his way to market, and
fetch her on Sunday evening, so that she should
be ready for school next day. So Milly-Molly-
Mandy would spend a whole night away from
home, which was very exciting to think of. But
just a day or two before she was to go Mother
received a letter from her friend to say she was
so sorry, but she couldn't have Milly-Molly-
Mandy after all, as a married son and his wife

had come unexpectedly to pay her a visit.

Milly-Molly-Mandy had to try very hard not to feel dreadfully disappointed, for she had never been away from home by herself before, and she had been looking forward to it so much.

'Never mind, Milly-Molly-Mandy,' said Mother, when Saturday morning arrived and Milly-Molly-Mandy came down to breakfast looking rather solemn, 'there are nice things happening all the time, if you keep your eyes open to see them.'

Milly-Molly-Mandy said, 'Yes, Muvver,' in a small voice, as she took her seat, though it didn't seem just then as if anything could possibly happen as nice as going away to stay.

But while Father and Mother and Grandpa and Grandma and Uncle and Aunty and Milly-Molly-Mandy were at breakfast Mrs Moggs, who was little-friend-Susan's mother, came round in a great hurry without a hat. And Mrs Moggs told them how some friends, who had to go to the town on business, had offered her a seat in their gig. And as Mrs Moggs's mother lived there Mrs Moggs thought it was a nice opportunity to go and see her, only she didn't like leaving Susan alone all day, Mr Moggs being out at work.

So Milly-Molly-Mandy's mother said, 'Let her come round here, Mrs Moggs. Milly-Molly-Mandy would like to have her. And I don't suppose you'll be back till late, so she'd better spend the night here too.'

Milly-Molly-Mandy was pleased, and Mrs Moggs thanked them very much indeed, and they all wished Mrs Moggs a nice trip, and then Mrs Moggs ran back home to get ready.

'Where will Susan sleep? – in the spare

room?' asked Milly-Molly-Mandy, making haste to finish her breakfast.

'Yes,' said Mother, 'and you had better sleep there too, to keep her company.'

Milly-Molly-Mandy was very much pleased at that, for she had never slept in the spare room – her cot-bed was in one corner of Father's and Mother's room.

'Why, Muvver!' she said, 'I can't have a visit of my own, but I'll just be able to enjoy Susan's instead, shan't I? P'r'aps it'll be almost quite as nice!'

She helped to wash up the breakfast things, and to make the spare-room bed, and to dust.

And then she was just looking out of the window, thinking how nice it would be for Susan to wake up in the morning with a new view outside, when what did she see but little-friend-Susan herself, trudging along up the

road with a basket on one arm and her coat on
the other. So she ran down to the gate to
welcome her in.

And though Milly-Molly-Mandy and little-
friend-Susan met almost every day, and very
often spent the whole day together, somehow
it felt so different to think little-friend-Susan
was going to stay the night with Milly-Molly-
Mandy that they couldn't help giving an extra
skip or two after they had kissed each other.

Milly-Molly-Mandy took her to see Mother,
and then they went up to the spare room to
unpack little-friend-Susan's basket.

They put her nightgown and brush and comb
and toothbrush and slippers in their proper
places, and decided which sides of the bed they
were going to sleep – and they found each
wanted the side that the other one didn't,
which was nice – though of course Milly-

Unpacking little-friend-Susan's basket

Molly-Mandy would have given little-friend-Susan first choice, anyway.

Then Milly-Molly-Mandy showed little-friend-Susan round the room, and let her admire the fat silk pin-cushion on the dressing-table, and the hair-tidy that Aunty had painted, and the ornaments on the chest of drawers – the china dogs with the rough-feeling coats, and the little girl with the china lace skirt.

And while they were looking at the fretwork bracket which Father had made for Mother before they were married, Aunty came running up to say Uncle was just going to drive to market, and they might go with him if they were quick.

So they scrambled into their coats and hats, and Milly-Molly-Mandy ran to ask Mother in a whisper if she might take a penny from her money-box to spend in town. And soon they were sitting up close together beside Uncle in the high pony-trap, while the little brown pony (whose name was Twinkletoes) trotted briskly along the white road.

Little-friend-Susan hadn't been for many drives. Milly-Molly-Mandy often went, but she enjoyed this one much more than usual, because little-friend-Susan was so interested and pleased with everything.

Billy Blunt was whipping a top outside his father's corn-shop as they drove through the village. They waved to him, and he waved back. And a little farther on Miss Muggins's niece, Jilly, was wheeling her doll's pram along the pavement, and called out, 'Hello, Milly-Molly-Mandy! Hello, Susan!'

And then they drove along a road through cornfields, where the little green blades of wheat were busy growing up to make big loaves of bread – which is why you must never interrupt them by walking in the corn, even if you see a poppy.

When they came to the town there were crowds of people everywhere, shouting about the things they had to sell. And Milly-Molly-Mandy and little-friend-Susan followed Uncle about the market-place, looking at all the stalls of fruit and sweets and books and fish and clothes and a hundred other things.

Milly-Molly-Mandy spent her penny on a big

yellow sugar-stick for little-friend-Susan, who broke it carefully in two, and gave her half.

When Uncle had done his business he took them to have dinner at a place where all the tables had marble tops, which made such a sharp clatter unless you put your glass down very gently. There were crowds of people eating at other tables round about, and a lot of talking and clattering of cups and plates. It was very exciting. Little-friend-Susan was having a splendid holiday.

When they had finished Uncle paid the bill and led the way back to where Twinkletoes was waiting patiently, munching in his nosebag. And off they drove again, clippety-cloppety, with Uncle's parcels stowed under the seat.

And when they got near home it did seem queer for Milly-Molly-Mandy and little-friend-Susan to go straight past the Moggs's cottage and not have to stop and say good-bye to each other. They squeezed each other's hand all the rest of the way home to the nice white cottage with the thatched roof, because they felt so pleased.

When bedtime drew near they had their baths together, just as if they were sisters. And then Milly-Molly-Mandy in her red dressing-gown, and little-friend-Susan in Grandma's red shawl, sat in front of the fire on little stools (with Toby the dog on one side, and Topsy the cat on the other), while Mother made them each a lid-potato for their suppers.

First Mother took two well-baked potatoes out of the oven. Then she nearly cut the tops off them – but not quite. Then she scooped all the potato out of the skins and mashed it up with a little salt and a little pepper and a lot of

butter. And then she pushed it back into the
two potato-skins, and shut the tops like little
lids.

Then Milly-Molly-Mandy and little-friend-
Susan were given a mug of milk and a plate of
bread-and-butter, and one of the nice warm
lid-potatoes. And they opened the potato-lids
and ate out of them with little spoons.

They did enjoy their suppers.

And when the last bit was gone Mother said,
'Now, you two, I've set the candle in your
room, and I'll be up to fetch it in ten minutes.'

So Milly-Molly-Mandy and little-friend-Susan
kissed good-night to Father and Mother and

Grandpa and Grandma and Uncle and Aunty, and stroked Toby the dog and Topsy the cat. And then they went upstairs to bed, hopping and skipping all the way, because they were so pleased they were going to sleep together in the spare room.

And next day, when Mrs Moggs came round to tell how she had enjoyed her trip, and to fetch Susan, Milly-Molly-Mandy said, 'Thank you very much indeed, Mrs Moggs, for Susan's visit. I have enjoyed it!'

Chapter Seven

Milly-Molly-Mandy Goes Gardening

Once upon a time, one Saturday morning, Milly-Molly-Mandy went down to the village. She had to go to Mr Blunt's corn-shop to order a list of things for Uncle – and would Mr Blunt please send them on Monday without fail?

Mr Blunt said, 'Surely, surely! Tell your uncle he shall have them first thing in the morning.'

And then Milly-Molly-Mandy, who loved the smell of the corn-shop, peeped into the great bins, and dug her hands down into the maize and bran and oats and let them sift through her fingers. And then she said good-bye and came out.

As she passed the Blunts' little garden at the side of the shop she saw Billy Blunt's back, bending down just the other side of the palings. It looked very busy.

Billy Blunt was a little bigger than Milly-Molly-Mandy, and she did not know him very well, but they always said 'Hullo!' when they met.

So Milly-Molly-Mandy peeped through the palings and said, 'Hullo, Billy!'

Billy Blunt looked round for a moment and said, 'Hullo!' And then he turned back to his work.

But he didn't say, 'Hullo, Milly-Molly-Mandy!' and he didn't smile. So Milly-Molly-Mandy stuck her toes in the fence and hung on and looked over the top.

'What's the matter?' Milly-Molly-Mandy asked.

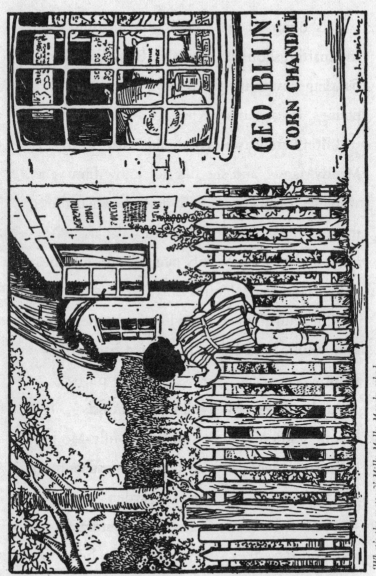

'What's the matter?' Milly-Molly-Mandy asked

Billy Blunt looked round again. 'Nothing's the matter,' he said gloomily. 'Only I've got to weed these old flower-beds right up to the house.'

'I don't mind weeding,' said Milly-Molly-Mandy.

'Huh! You try it here, and see how you like it!' said Billy Blunt. 'The earth's as hard as nails, and the weeds have got roots pretty near a mile long.'

Milly-Molly-Mandy wasn't quite sure whether he meant it as an invitation, but anyhow she accepted it as one, and pushed open the little white gate and came into the Blunts' garden.

It was a nice garden, smelling of wallflowers.

Billy Blunt said, 'There's a garden-fork.' So Milly-Molly-Mandy took it up and started work on the other side of the flower-bed which bordered the little brick path up to the house. And they dug away together.

Presently Milly-Molly-Mandy said, 'Doesn't the earth smell nice when you turn it up?'

And Billy Blunt said, 'Does it? Yes, it does rather.' And they went on weeding.

Presently Milly-Molly-Mandy, pulling tufts of grass out of the pansies, asked, 'What do you do this for, if you don't like it?'

And Billy Blunt, tugging at a dandelion root, grunted and said, 'Father says I ought to be making myself useful.'

'That's our sort of fruit,' said Milly-Molly-Mandy. 'My Muvver says we'd be like

apple-trees which didn't grow apples if we didn't be useful.'

'Huh!' said Billy Blunt. 'Funny idea, us growing fruit! Never thought of it like that.' And they went on weeding.

Presently Milly-Molly-Mandy asked, 'Why're there all those little holes in the lawn?'

'Dad's been digging out dandelions,' said Billy Blunt. 'He wants to make the garden nice.'

Then Milly-Molly-Mandy said, 'There's lots of grass here, only it oughtn't to be. We might plant it in the holes.'

'Umm!' said Billy Blunt, 'and then we'll be making the lawn look as tidy as the beds. Let's!'

So they dug, and they turned the earth, and they pulled out what didn't belong there. And all the weeds they threw into a heap to be burned, and all the tufts of grass they carefully planted in the lawn. And after a time the flower-beds began to look most beautifully neat, and you could see hardly any bald places on the lawn.

Presently Mr Blunt came out of the shop on to the pavement. He had a can of green paint and a brush in his hand, and he reached over the palings and set them down among the daisies on the lawn.

'Hullo, Milly-Molly-Mandy!' said Mr Blunt. 'Thought you'd gone home. Well, you two have been doing good work on those beds there. Billy, I'm going to paint the water-butt and the handle of the roller some time. Perhaps you'd like to do it for me? You'll have to clean off the rust first with sandpaper.'

Billy Blunt and Milly-Molly-Mandy looked quite eager.

Billy Blunt said, 'Rather, Dad!' And Milly-Molly-Mandy looked with great interest at the green can and the garden-roller. But she knew she ought to be starting back to dinner at the nice white cottage with the thatched roof, or Father and Mother and Grandpa and Grandma and Uncle and Aunty would be wondering what had become of her. So she handed her garden-fork back to Billy Blunt and walked slowly to the gate.

But Billy Blunt said, 'Couldn't you come again after dinner? I'll save you some of the painting.'

So Milly-Molly-Mandy gave a little skip and said 'I'd like to, if Muvver doesn't want me.'

So after dinner, when she had helped with the washing-up, Milly-Molly-Mandy ran hoppity-skip all the way down to the village again. And there in the Blunts' garden was Billy

Blunt, busy rubbing the iron bands on the
water-butt with a sheet of sandpaper.

'Hullo, Billy!' said Milly-Molly-Mandy.

'Hullo, Milly-Molly-Mandy!' said Billy Blunt.
He looked very hot and dirty, but he smiled
quite broadly. And then he said, 'I've saved the
garden-roller for you to paint – it's all
sandpapered ready.'

Milly-Molly-Mandy thought that was nice of
Billy Blunt, for the sandpapering was the nasty,
dirty part of the work.

Billy Blunt got the lid off the can, and stirred
up the beautiful green paint with a stick. Then
all by himself he thought of fetching a piece of
newspaper to pin over her frock to keep her
clean. And then he went back to rubbing the
water-butt, while Milly-Molly-Mandy dipped the
brush carefully into the lovely full can of green
paint, and started work on the lawn mower.

The handle had a pattern in wriggly bits of iron, and it was great fun getting the paint into all the cracks. And you can't imagine how beautiful and new that roller looked when the paint was on it.

Billy Blunt had to keep leaving his water-butt to see how it was going on, because the wriggly bits looked so nice when they were green, and he hadn't any wriggly bits on his water-butt.

By the end of the afternoon you ought to have seen how nice the garden looked! The flower-beds were clean and trim, the lawn tidied up, the water-butt stood glistening green by the side of the house, and the roller lay glistening green on the grass.

And when Mr Blunt came out and saw it all he was pleased!

He called Mrs Blunt, and Mrs Blunt was pleased too. She gave them each a banana, and they ate them sitting on one of the corn-bins in the shop.

And afterwards Billy Blunt buried Milly-Molly-Mandy in the corn, right up to the neck. And when he helped her out again she was all bits of corn, down her neck, and in her socks, and on her hair. But Milly-Molly-Mandy didn't mind a scrap. She liked it.

Chapter Eight

Milly-Molly-Mandy Makes a Cosy

Once upon a time Milly-Molly-Mandy went out visiting, in her best hat and new shoes and white cotton gloves. Milly-Molly-Mandy felt very proper indeed. She walked down the road, past the Moggs's cottage, past Mr Blunt's corn-shop, till she came to Miss Muggins's small shop. For Milly-Molly-Mandy was going to tea with Miss Muggins and her little niece, Jilly.

Miss Muggins's shop and the passage behind smelt so interesting – like calico and flannelette and brown paper, with faint whiffs of peppermint and raspberry-drops. (For Miss

Muggins sold a few sweets too, from bottles on a shelf in her window.)

But the little sitting-room at the back of the shop smelt mostly of warm buttered scones and sugary cakes, for the table was all laid ready, and Miss Muggins and Jilly were waiting for her. And over the teapot in front of Miss Muggins was a most beautiful cosy, all made of odd-shaped pieces of bright-coloured silks and velvets, with loops of coloured cord on top. Milly-Molly-Mandy did like it!

After Milly-Molly-Mandy had eaten two buttered scones she couldn't help saying, 'Isn't that a beautiful cosy!'

And Jilly said, 'Aunty made it!'

Milly-Molly-Mandy thought how nice it would be to have such a beautiful cosy on the table at home.

When she had eaten a pink sugary cake

she said, 'Wasn't that cosy very difficult to make?'

And Miss Muggins (who had just come back from serving a lady with a card of linen buttons and some black elastic) said, 'Oh, no, it was quite easy! You ought to get your aunty to teach you feather-stitching, Milly-Molly-Mandy, so that you could make one!'

Milly-Molly-Mandy thought how nice it would be to make Mother such a beautiful cosy, but she didn't know how she could get the stuffs.

After the meal she played with Jilly and her dolls' house, and when it was time to go Miss Muggins came out of the shop with a small piece of bright red satin, to start Milly-Molly-Mandy making a cosy. Milly-Molly-Mandy was pleased!

Then she thanked Miss Muggins very much

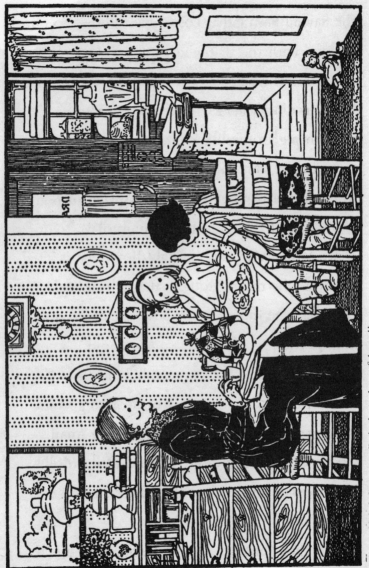

She couldn't help saying, 'Isn't that a beautiful cosy!'

for having her, and ran home to the nice white cottage with the thatched roof.

She hid the red satin in her doll's cradle, and wondered a great deal how she could get enough pieces of stuff to make a cosy.

And then, one morning, Mother turned out of her piece-bag some scraps of green ribbon, and said Milly-Molly-Mandy might have them. Milly-Molly-Mandy *was* pleased!

But as she didn't like the thought of Mother giving anything for her own secret present she looked round for something she could do in exchange for it. And she saw, behind the kitchen door, a muddy pair of Mother's shoes waiting to be cleaned. So Milly-Molly-Mandy quietly got out the boot-box and cleaned them.

So now Milly-Molly-Mandy had some red pieces and some green pieces.

And then, one afternoon, Father gave her a

penny to buy some sweets. And Milly-Molly-Mandy said, 'Would you mind, Farver, if I bought something else instead, for a great secret!'

And Father didn't mind, so Milly-Molly-Mandy went to Miss Muggins's shop and bought a skein of black silk to do the feather-stitching with.

So now Milly-Molly-Mandy had some red pieces and some green pieces and a skein of black silk.

And then, one day, Grandma altered her best dress, which was of velvet, and the part she cut off she gave to Milly-Molly-Mandy to play with.

So now Milly-Molly-Mandy had some red pieces and some green pieces and a skein of black silk and some black pieces.

And then, one morning, Grandpa let her

come with him in the pony-trap to the town. And while they were there he looked at the shop windows and asked Milly-Molly-Mandy what she would like for a little present. And Milly-Molly-Mandy said, 'Oh, Grandpa, could I have some coloured cord for a great secret?' So Grandpa bought her some coloured cord without asking any questions.

So now Milly-Molly-Mandy had some red pieces and some green pieces and a skein of black silk and some black pieces and some coloured cord.

And then, one afternoon, Aunty was retrimming a hat, and when she took off the old lavender ribbon it had on it she said Milly-Molly-Mandy could have it. And Milly-Molly-Mandy found some parts of it were quite good.

So now Milly-Molly-Mandy had some red pieces and some green pieces and a skein of black silk and some black pieces and some coloured cord and some lavender pieces.

And then, one day, Uncle was turning over the neckties in his drawer, and there was one blue one with yellow spots which Uncle didn't like, and he threw it to Milly-Molly-Mandy, saying, 'Here, Milly-Molly-Mandy, this'll do for a doll's sash, or something.'

So now Milly-Molly-Mandy had some red pieces and some green pieces and a skein of black silk and some black pieces and some coloured cord and some lavender pieces and some blue pieces with yellow spots.

And Milly-Molly-Mandy thought she really had enough now to begin the cosy!

She went to Aunty and asked if she would kindly teach her to do feather-stitching for a great secret. So Aunty showed her how to cut up the pieces and feather-stitch them together.

And then, for weeks, Milly-Molly-Mandy
spent nearly all her spare time in the attic or
in the barn, sewing and sewing, and never
showed anyone but Aunty what she was doing.

One evening Father said, 'Whatever is Milly-
Molly-Mandy up to these days?'

And Mother said, 'I can't think.'

And Grandpa said, 'I haven't seen her
properly for days.'

And Grandma said, 'I think she's got some
kind of a secret on.'

And Uncle said, 'I shouldn't be surprised.'

But Aunty said nothing at all, and only put
the tablecloth straight.

And then, just when Mother had finished

laying the supper, Milly-Molly-Mandy came in with a very pink face and her hands behind her back.

Mother went to the oven to bring out a plate of hot potato-cakes. And when she turned round again, there, at her end of the table, was the most beautiful patchwork cosy keeping the cocoa-jug hot!

'Milly-Molly-Mandy!' said Mother.

She hurried to her place, while Milly-Molly-Mandy jumped up and down, and Father and Grandpa and Grandma and Uncle and Aunty all looked on admiringly.

'Oh, Milly-Molly-Mandy!' said Mother, 'what
— a — *beautiful* — cosy!'

And Mother was so pleased, and Milly-
Molly-Mandy was so glad she was pleased, that
they just had to hug and kiss each other very
hard indeed.

And the potato-cakes got almost cold, but
the cocoa was just as hot as hot!

Chapter Nine

Milly-Molly-Mandy Keeps Shop

Once upon a time Milly-Molly-Mandy was walking home from school with some little friends – Billy Blunt, Miss Muggins's niece Jilly, and, of course, little-friend-Susan. And they were all talking about what they would like to do when they were big.

Billy Blunt said he would have a motor-bus and drive people to the station and pull their boxes about. Miss Muggins's Jilly said she would curl her hair and be a lady who acts for the pictures. Little-friend-Susan wanted to be a nurse with long white streamers, and push a pram with two babies in it.

Milly-Molly-Mandy wanted a shop like Miss Muggins, where she could sell sweets, and cut pretty coloured stuff for people's dresses with a big pair of scissors. And 'Oh, dear!' said Milly-Molly-Mandy, 'I wish we didn't have to wait till we had growed up!'

Then they came to Miss Muggins's shop, and Jilly said 'Good-bye,' and went in.

And then they came to Mr Blunt's corn-shop, which was only a few steps farther on, and Billy Blunt said 'Good-bye,' and went in.

And then Milly-Molly-Mandy and little-friend-Susan, with their arms round each other, walked up the white road with the

fields each side till they came to the Moggs's
cottage, and little-friend-Susan said 'Good-
bye' and went in.

And Milly-Molly-Mandy went hoppity-
skipping on alone till she came to the nice
white cottage with the thatched roof, where
Mother was at the gate to meet her.

Next day was Saturday, and Milly-Molly-
Mandy went down to the village on an errand
for Mother. And when she had done it she saw
Miss Muggins standing at her shop door,
looking rather worried.

And when Miss Muggins saw Milly-Molly-
Mandy she said, 'Oh, Milly-Molly-Mandy,
would you mind running to ask Mrs Jakes if
she could come and mind my shop for an
hour? Tell her I've got to go to see someone on
very important business, and I don't know
what to do, and Jilly's gone picnicking.'

So Milly-Molly-Mandy ran to ask Mrs Jakes.
But Mrs Jakes said, 'Tell Miss Muggins I'm
very sorry, but I've just got the cakes in the
oven, and I can't leave them.'

So Milly-Molly-Mandy ran back and told
Miss Muggins, and Miss Muggins said, 'I
wonder if Mrs Blunt would come.'

So Milly-Molly-Mandy ran to ask Mrs Blunt.
But Mrs Blunt said, 'I'm sorry, but I'm simply
up to my eyes in house-cleaning, and I can't
leave just now.'

So Milly-Molly-Mandy ran back and told
Miss Muggins, and Miss Muggins said she
didn't know of anyone else she could ask.

Then Milly-Molly-Mandy said, 'Oh, Miss
Muggins, couldn't I look after the shop for you?
I'll tell people you'll be back in an hour, and if
they only want a sugar-stick or something I
could give it them – I know how much it is!'

Miss Muggins looked at Milly-Molly-Mandy, and then she said, 'Well, you aren't very big, but I know you're careful, Milly-Molly-Mandy.'

So she gave her lots of instructions about asking people if they would come back in an hour, and not selling things unless she was quite sure of the price, and so on. And then Miss Muggins put on her hat and feather boa and hurried off.

And Milly-Molly-Mandy was left alone in charge of the shop!

Milly-Molly-Mandy felt very solemn and careful indeed. She dusted the counter with a duster which she saw hanging on a nail; and then she peeped into the window at all the handkerchiefs and socks and bottles of sweets – and she could see Mrs Hubble arranging the loaves and cakes in her shop-window opposite, and Mr Smale (who had the grocer's shop with

a little counter at the back where you posted
parcels and bought stamps and letter-paper)
standing at his door enjoying the sunshine. And
Milly-Molly-Mandy felt so pleased that she had
a shop as well as they.

And then, suddenly, the door-handle rattled,
and the little bell over the door jangle-jangled
up and down, and who should come in but
little-friend-Susan! – And how little-friend-
Susan did stare when she saw Milly-Molly-
Mandy behind the counter!

'Miss Muggins has gone out on 'portant
business, but she'll be back in an hour. What
do you want?' said Milly-Molly-Mandy.

'A packet of safety-pins for Mother. What
are you doing here?' said little-friend-Susan.

'I'm looking after the shop,' said Milly-
Molly-Mandy. 'And I know where the safety-
pins are, because I had to buy some yesterday.'

So Milly-Molly-Mandy wrapped up the safety-pins in a piece of thin brown paper, and twisted the end just as Miss Muggins did. And she handed the packet to little-friend-Susan, and little-friend-Susan handed her a penny.

And then little-friend-Susan wanted to stay and play 'shops' with Milly-Molly-Mandy.

But Milly-Molly-Mandy shook her head solemnly and said, 'No, this isn't play; it's business. I've got to be very, very careful. You'd better go, Susan.'

And just then the bell jangled again, and a lady came in, so little-friend-Susan went out. (She peered through the window for a time to see how Milly-Molly-Mandy got on, but Milly-Molly-Mandy wouldn't look at her.)

The lady was Miss Bloss, who lived opposite, over the baker's shop, with Mrs Bloss. She wanted a quarter of a yard of pink flannelette,

because she was making a wrapper for her
mother, and she hadn't bought quite enough
for the collar. She said she didn't like to waste
a whole hour till Miss Muggins returned.

Milly-Molly-Mandy stood on one leg and
wondered what to do, and Miss Bloss tapped
with one finger and wondered what to do.

And then Miss Bloss said, 'That's the roll my
flannelette came off. I'm quite sure Miss
Muggins wouldn't mind my taking some.'

So between them they measured off the pink
flannelette, and Milly-Molly-Mandy fetched
Miss Muggins's big scissors, and Miss Bloss
made a crease exactly where the quarter-yard
came; and Milly-Molly-Mandy breathed very
hard and cut slowly and carefully right along
the crease to the end.

And then she wrapped the piece up and gave
it to Miss Bloss, and Miss Bloss handed her half

a crown, saying, 'Ask Miss Muggins to send me the change when she gets back.'

And then Miss Bloss went out.

And then for a time nobody came in, and Milly-Molly-Mandy amused herself by trying to find the rolls of stuff that different people's dresses had come off. There was her own pink-and-white-striped cotton (looking so lovely and new) and Mother's blue-checked apron stuff and Mrs Jakes's Sunday gown . . .

Then rattle went the handle and jangle went the bell, and who should come in but Billy Blunt!

'I'm Miss Muggins,' said Milly-Molly-Mandy. 'What do you want to buy?'

'Where's Miss Muggins?' said Billy Blunt.

So Milly-Molly-Mandy had to explain again. And then Billy Blunt said he had wanted a penny-worth of aniseed-balls. So Milly-Molly-

'I'm Miss Muggins. What do you want to buy?'

Mandy stood on a box and reached down the glass jar from the shelf.

They were twelve a penny she knew, for she had often bought them. So she counted them out, and then Billy Blunt counted them.

And Billy Blunt said, 'You've got one too many here.'

So Milly-Molly-Mandy counted again, and she found one too many too. So they dropped one back in the jar, and Milly-Molly-Mandy put the others into a little bag and swung it over by the corners, just as Miss Muggins did, and gave it to Billy Blunt. And Billy Blunt gave her his penny.

And then Billy Blunt grinned, and said, 'Good morning, ma'am.'

And Milly-Molly-Mandy said, 'Good morning, sir,' and Billy Blunt went out.

After that an hour began to seem rather a long time, with the sun shining so outside. But at last the little bell gave a lively jangle again, and Miss Muggins had returned!

And though Milly-Molly-Mandy had enjoyed herself very much, she thought perhaps, after all, she would rather wait until she was grown up before she kept a shop for herself.

Chapter Ten

Milly-Molly-Mandy Gives a Party

Once upon a time Milly-Molly-Mandy had a plan. And when she had thought over the plan for a while she went to look in her money-box. And in the money-box were four pennies and a ha'penny, which Milly-Molly-Mandy did not think would be enough for her plan. So Milly-Molly-Mandy went off to talk it over with little-friend-Susan down the road.

'Susan,' said Milly-Molly-Mandy, 'I've got a plan (only it's a great secret). I want to give a party in our barn to Farver and Muvver and Grandpa and Grandma and Uncle and Aunty. And I want to buy refreshments. And you and I will be waitresses. And if there's anything over we can eat it up afterwards.'

Little-friend-Susan thought it a very good plan indeed.

'Will we wear caps?' she asked.

'Yes,' said Milly-Molly-Mandy, 'and aprons. Only I haven't got enough money for the refreshments, so I don't think there'll be any over. We must think.'

So Milly-Molly-Mandy and little-friend-Susan sat down and thought hard.

'We must work and earn some,' said Milly-Molly-Mandy.

'But how?' said little-friend-Susan.

'We might sell something,' said Milly-Molly-Mandy.

'But what?' said little-friend-Susan. So they had to think some more.

Presently Milly-Molly-Mandy said, 'I've got

pansies and marigolds in my garden.'

And little-friend-Susan said, 'I've got nasturtiums in mine.'

'We could run errands for people,' said Milly-Molly-Mandy.

'And clean brass,' said little-friend-Susan.

That was a lovely idea, so Milly-Molly-Mandy fetched a pencil and paper and wrote out very carefully:

Millicent Margaret Amanda & Susan & Co. have bunches of flowers for sale and clean brass very cheap (we do not spill the polish) and run errands very cheap.

'What's "and Co."?' said little-friend-Susan.

'It's just business,' said Milly-Molly-Mandy, 'but perhaps we might ask Billy Blunt to be it. And he could be a waiter.'

Then they hung the notice on the front gate,

and waited just the other side of the hedge.

Several people passed, but nobody seemed to want anything. Then at last a motor-car came along with a lady and gentleman in it; and when they saw the nice white cottage with the thatched roof they stopped at the gate to ask if they could get some cream there.

Milly-Molly-Mandy said, 'I'll go and ask Muvver,' and took the little pot they held out. And when she came back with it full of cream the lady and gentleman had read the notice and were asking little-friend-Susan questions. As the lady paid for the cream she said they must certainly have some flowers. So they each bought a bunch. And then the gentleman said the round brass thing in front of his car needed cleaning very badly – could the firm do it straight away?

So Milly-Molly-Mandy said, 'Yes, sir,' and

raced back to the cottage to give Mother the
cream-money and to borrow the brass-
polishing box. And then she cleaned the round
brass thing in front of the car with one piece
of cloth and little-friend-Susan rubbed it bright
with another piece of cloth, and the lady and
gentleman looked on and seemed very satisfied.

Then the gentleman asked 'How much?' and
paid them twopence for the flowers and a
penny for the polishing. Milly-Molly-Mandy
wanted to do some more polishing for the
money, but the gentleman said they couldn't
stop. And then they said good-bye and went
off, and the lady turned and waved, and Milly-
Molly-Mandy and little-friend-Susan waved
back until they were gone.

Milly-Molly-Mandy and little-friend-Susan
felt very happy and pleased.

And now they had sevenpence-ha'penny for

the refreshments. Father and Mother and Grandpa and Grandma and Uncle and Aunty and Mrs Moggs, little-friend-Susan's mother, made seven.

Then who should look over the hedge but Mr Jakes, the Postman, on his way home from collecting letters from the letter-boxes. He had seen the notice on the gate.

'What's this? You trying to make a fortune?' said the Postman.

'Yes,' said Milly-Molly-Mandy, 'we've earned threepence!'

'My! And what do you plan to do with it?' said the Postman.

'We've got a secret!' said Milly-Molly-Mandy, with a little skip.

'Ah!' said the Postman, 'I guess it's a nice one, too!'

Milly-Molly-Mandy looked at little-friend-

Susan, and then she looked at the Postman. He was a nice Postman. 'You won't tell if we tell you?' she asked.

'Try me!' said the Postman promptly. So Milly-Molly-Mandy told him they were planning to give a party to Father and Mother and Grandpa and Grandma and Uncle and Aunty and Mrs Moggs.

'They're in luck, they are!' said the Postman. 'Nobody asks me to parties.'

Milly-Molly-Mandy looked at little-friend-Susan again, and then she looked at the Postman. He was a very nice Postman. Then she said, 'Supposing you were invited, would you come?'

'You try me!' said the Postman promptly again. And then he hitched up his letter-bag and went on.

'Farver and Muvver and Grandpa and

Grandma and Uncle and Aunty and Mrs Moggs and the Postman. We've got to earn some more,' said Milly-Molly-Mandy. 'Let's go down to the village and ask Billy Blunt to be "and Co.," and p'r'aps he'll have an idea.'

Billy Blunt was in the road outside the corn-shop, mending the handles of his box on wheels. He had made it nearly all himself, and it was a very nice one, painted green like the water-butt and the lawn-roller. He thought 'and Co.' was rather a funny name, but said he would be it all right, and offered to make them a box with a slit in it, where they could keep their earnings. And he put in four farthings out of his collection. (Billy Blunt was collecting farthings – he had nineteen in an empty bird-seed bag.)

So now they had eightpence-ha'penny for the refreshments.

On Monday morning, on their way home to dinner, Milly-Molly-Mandy and little-friend-Susan passed Mrs Jakes, the Postman's wife, at her door, getting a breath of fresh air before dishing up her dinner. And Mrs Jakes said, 'Good morning! How's the firm of Millicent Margaret Amanda, Susan, and Co. getting on?'

Milly-Molly-Mandy said, 'Very well, thank you!'

'My husband's told me about your brass-cleaning,' said Mrs Jakes. 'I've got a whole mantelshelf full that wants doing!'

Milly-Molly-Mandy and little-friend-Susan were very pleased, and arranged to come in directly school was over in the afternoon and clean it.

And they cleaned a mug and three candlesticks and two lamps – one big and one

little – and a tray and a warming-pan, and they
didn't spill or waste any of the polish. Mrs
Jakes seemed very satisfied, and gave them
each a penny and a piece of cake.

So now they had tenpence-ha'penny for
refreshments.

But when they got outside Milly-Molly-
Mandy said, 'Farver and Muvver and Grandpa
and Grandma and Uncle and Aunty and Mrs
Moggs and the Postman and Mrs Postman –
I wonder if we've earned enough, Susan!'

As they turned home they passed the forge,
and of course they had to stop a moment at
the doorway, as usual, to watch the fire

roaring, and Mr Rudge the Blacksmith banging with his hammer on the anvil.

Little-friend-Susan was just a bit nervous of the Blacksmith – he was so big, and his face was so dirty it made his teeth look very white and his eyes very twinkly when he smiled at them. But Milly-Molly-Mandy knew he was nice and clean under the dirt, which he couldn't help while he worked. So she smiled back.

And the Blacksmith said, 'Hullo!'

And Milly-Molly-Mandy said, 'Hullo!'

Then the Blacksmith beckoned with his finger and said, 'Come here!'

Milly-Molly-Mandy gave a little jump, and little-friend-Susan pulled at her hand, but Milly-Molly-Mandy knew he was really just a nice man under the dirt, so she went up to him.

And the Blacksmith said, 'Look what I've got here!' And he showed them a tiny little horseshoe, just like a proper one, only smaller, which he had made for them to keep. Milly-Molly-Mandy and little-friend-Susan were pleased!

Milly-Molly-Mandy thanked him very much. And then she looked at the Blacksmith and said, 'If you were invited to a party, would you come?'

And the Blacksmith looked at Milly-Molly-Mandy with twinkly eyes and said he'd come quite fast – so long as it wasn't before five o'clock on Saturday, when he was playing cricket with his team in the meadow.

When they got outside again Milly-Molly-Mandy said, 'Farver and Muvver and Grandpa and Grandma and Uncle and Aunty and Mrs Moggs and the Postman and Mrs Postman and the Blacksmith. We'll ask them for half-past five, and we ought to earn some more money, Susan!'

Just then they met Billy Blunt coming along, pulling his box on wheels with a bundle in it. And Billy Blunt grinned and said, 'I'm fetching Mrs Bloss's washing, for the firm!' Milly-Molly-Mandy and little-friend-Susan were pleased!

When Saturday morning came all the invitations had been given out, and the firm of Millicent Margaret Amanda, Susan, and Co. was very busy putting things tidy in the barn, and covering up things which couldn't be moved with lots of green branches which Grandpa was trimming from the hedges.

And when half-past five came Milly-Molly-Mandy and little-friend-Susan, with clean hands and paper caps and aprons, waited by the barn

door to welcome the guests. And each
gentleman received a marigold buttonhole, and
each lady a pansy.

Everybody arrived in good time, except the
Blacksmith, who was just a bit late – he looked
so clean and pink in his white cricket-flannels,
Milly-Molly-Mandy hardly knew him – and
Billy Blunt. But Billy Blunt came lugging a
gramophone and two records which he had
borrowed from a bigger boy at school. (He
never told, but he had given the boy all the
rest of his collection of farthings – fifteen of
them, which makes three-pence-three-farthings
– in exchange.)

Then Billy Blunt, who didn't want to dance,
looked after the gramophone, while Father and
Mother and Grandpa and Grandma and Uncle
and Aunty and Mrs Moggs and the Postman
and Mrs Postman and the Blacksmith and

Milly-Molly-Mandy and little-friend-Susan danced together in the old barn till the dust flew. And Milly-Molly-Mandy danced a lot with the Blacksmith as well as with everybody else, and so did little-friend-Susan.

They did enjoy themselves!

And then there were refreshments – raspberry-drops and aniseed-balls on saucers trimmed with little flowers; and late blackberries on leaf plates; and sherbet drinks, which Billy Blunt prepared while Milly-Molly-Mandy and little-friend-Susan stood by to tell people just the very moment to drink, when it was fizzing properly. (It was exciting!) And a jelly which Milly-Molly-Mandy and little-friend-Susan had made themselves from a packet, only it had to be eaten rather like soup, as it wouldn't stand up properly.

But Father and Mother and Grandpa and

And then there were refreshments

Grandma and Uncle and Aunty and Mrs Moggs
and the Postman and Mrs Postman and the
Blacksmith all said they had never enjoyed a
jelly so much. And the Blacksmith, in a big
voice, proposed a vote of thanks to the firm
for the delightful party and refreshments, and
everybody else said 'Hear! hear!' and clapped.
And Milly-Molly-Mandy and little-friend-Susan
joined in the clapping too, which wasn't quite
proper, but they were so happy they couldn't
help it!

And then all the guests went home.

And when the firm came to clear up the
refreshments they found there was only one
aniseed-ball left. But placed among the empty

saucers and glasses on the bench were a small
basket of pears and a bag of mixed sweets with
a ticket 'For the Waiter and Waitresses' on it!

Chapter Eleven

Milly-Molly-Mandy Goes Visiting

Once upon a time Milly-Molly-Mandy had a
letter. It was from Mrs Hooker, who had been
a friend of Mother's ever since she was a little
girl. And it said how sorry Mrs Hooker was to
have to put Milly-Molly-Mandy off last time
she had invited her – that time Milly-Molly-
Mandy had enjoyed little-friend-Susan's visit
instead of her own. But now Mrs Hooker's son
and his wife had gone abroad to live, and Mrs
Hooker would be very pleased if Mother
would let Milly-Molly-Mandy come and spend
a weekend with her, as promised.

Milly-Molly-Mandy was very pleased, and

Father and Mother and Grandpa and Grandma
and Uncle and Aunty were very pleased for
her. They talked of Milly-Molly-Mandy going
away nearly all supper-time, and Aunty
promised to put a new ribbon round her best
hat, and Mother said she must make her a very
nice 'going-away' nightdress in a case, and
Uncle said he would feel very honoured if she
were to borrow his small leather bag to take it
in, and Father gave her sixpence to put in her
purse.

Milly-Molly-Mandy felt so excited!

When Saturday morning came Grandpa got
the pony-trap ready to go to market as usual,
and Milly-Molly-Mandy came skipping down
the path, ready to go with him and meet Mrs

Hooker as arranged. Her hat looked just like new, and she had on a pair of nice warm woolly gloves that Grandma had knitted for her, and Aunty's best nice warm woolly scarf, lent for the occasion.

Mother gave her a bunch of late chrysanthemums and a cream cheese for Mrs Hooker, with her love. And then Grandpa got up in the trap and took the reins, and Milly-Molly-Mandy was lifted up beside him. Then off trotted Twinkletoes, and Father and Mother and Grandma and Uncle and Aunty called, 'Good-bye, Milly-Molly-Mandy! Have a nice time!' and waved, and Milly-Molly-Mandy waved back till she couldn't see them any longer. And she was really off for her visit!

They didn't see little-friend-Susan or Billy Blunt as they drove through the village, but Milly-Molly-Mandy waved at their houses, in

case they might see her. And then they were
out in the open country, and Milly-Molly-
Mandy was glad of Aunty's nice warm woolly
scarf and her own nice warm woolly gloves.

They came to the town, and got down by
the big clock in the market-place, and Mrs
Hooker came hurrying up, looking quite
different, somehow (for Milly-Molly-Mandy
had seen her only once before, and had nearly
forgotten what she looked like).

And then Grandpa kissed Milly-Molly-Mandy
good-bye, and went off to do his business in
the market. And Milly-Molly-Mandy took Mrs
Hooker's hand in its grey kid glove, and went
off with her.

Milly-Molly-Mandy had never been away
from home to stay before without either Father
or Mother or Grandpa or Grandma or Uncle
or Aunty, and it felt so strange and exciting.

'Well, Milly-Molly-Mandy,' said Mrs Hooker, 'I just want to buy some crochet-cotton, and then we will be getting home.'

So they went into a big draper's shop, heaps of times bigger than Miss Muggins's shop at home, and Mrs Hooker asked for crochet-cotton. And while she was buying it Milly-Molly-Mandy looked about and felt the purse in her pocket. Presently she saw some pretty little guards to put over the points of knitting-needles, which she thought would be so useful to Grandma.

And suddenly Milly-Molly-Mandy had an idea: What fun it would be to take presents home for everybody! She had five pennies of her own as well as the sixpence Father had given her.

She wondered what everybody would like, and remembered Mother once saying,

'Good-bye, Milly-Molly-Mandy! Have a nice time!'

'Handkerchiefs always make an acceptable present.' So when she had bought the guards for Grandma she asked the lady behind the counter if she had some handkerchiefs that weren't at all expensive, and the lady behind the counter brought out a boxful, each one marked with a letter in one corner. So Milly-Molly-Mandy looked at them all, and chose one for Mother with 'M' in the corner, and one for Aunty with 'A' in the corner. And then she had only two pennies left. She wondered whatever she could get for Father and Grandpa and Uncle with twopence.

Presently Mrs Hooker finished her purchases, and they went out into the street to go to Mrs Hooker's house. There were such a lot of people, all over the pavement and road, for it was market-day, and there seemed so much to look at that Milly-Molly-Mandy wished she had a dozen pairs of eyes. But still, with only two, she managed to keep one on the shop-windows as they passed, hoping to see something which Father and Grandpa and Uncle might like. And suddenly she saw a tray of pink sugar mice in a sweet-shop, labelled 'Two a penny'.

'Oh, Mrs Hooker!' said Milly-Molly-Mandy, 'would you mind waiting a moment while I get a sugar mouse to take home to Farver and Grandpa and Uncle?'

So Mrs Hooker held the leather bag and chrysanthemums and cream cheese until Milly-Molly-Mandy came out with a bag of sugar mice in her hand (she had bought four, and one was to be a good-bye present for Mrs Hooker). She wished she could get presents for little-friend-Susan and Billy Blunt, but that didn't seem possible, for she had used up all her money.

When they got to Mrs Hooker's house they put the chrysanthemums in a vase on the table, and the cream cheese in a dish on the sideboard. (Mrs Hooker was very pleased with them.) And then there was just time before dinner for Milly-Molly-Mandy to unpack her small leather bag in the little room she was to sleep in all by herself. And she found Mother had popped in Booby Rabbit, the toy she had won at a party once, and had slept with ever since. She was so glad to see him, and hid him in her nightdress-case so that he shouldn't be seen, because he hadn't been invited. (It was such fun for Booby Rabbit!)

The plates at dinner were so pretty – quite different from the ones they had at home – and so were the wall-paper and the carpet. Altogether, there seemed so much to think about that there wasn't time to say much more than 'Yes, please,' and 'No, thank you.' But she enjoyed her dinner very much.

After dinner Mrs Hooker said, 'I have asked Milly next door to come and spend the afternoon with you, and you can play with my old toys.'

Milly-Molly-Mandy was very interested. And then she said, 'Will Milly-next-door put her hat and coat on to come here?' – for their nearest neighbours at home were little-friend-Susan and the Moggses, and they lived five minutes' walk down the road (but only three minutes if you ran).

Mrs Hooker said she really couldn't say. And presently the next-door gate squeaked, and then Mrs Hooker's gate squeaked, and then the door-bell rang, and Milly-next-door came in (with a coat on and no hat).

Mrs Hooker told Milly-Molly-Mandy to take Milly-next-door upstairs to her little room, to take her coat off. So Milly-Molly-Mandy played hostess, and let Milly-next-door use her comb, and asked her if her name was really Millicent Margaret Amanda, like Milly-Molly-Mandy's own. And Milly-next-door said no, it was Mildred.

Then Milly-next-door admired the new nightdress-case lying on the bed, and when Milly-Molly-Mandy showed her the new nightdress inside (which was pink) Milly-next-door admired that too. (She didn't see Booby Rabbit.) But when Milly-Molly-Mandy showed her the handkerchiefs marked 'M' for Mother and 'A' for Aunty, Milly-next-door was quite surprised.

'Oh,' said Milly-next-door, 'my mother never has her handkerchiefs marked "M"! She has them marked "R", because her other name's Rose. What's your mother's other name?'

'It's Polly,' said Milly-Molly-Mandy, in a sad little voice.

'Oh, well,' said Milly-next-door comfortingly, 'I expect they can use them, even if they aren't quite proper.'

But Milly-Molly-Mandy didn't feel very comforted, for she had so wanted to give Mother and Aunty proper presents.

Then they went downstairs and played all the afternoon with Mrs Hooker's funny old-fashioned toys. And when the lamps were lit Mrs Hooker brought out a beautiful paint-box and a fashion-paper full of little girls, and Milly-Molly-Mandy and Milly-next-door each painted a little girl very carefully, and cut it out with Mrs Hooker's scissors, and gave it to each other for a keepsake.

And during tea Milly-Molly-Mandy had another good idea: she would paint and cut out some paper dolls, very, very nicely, and take them home to little-friend-Susan for a present! Milly-Molly-Mandy didn't think Billy Blunt would care for paper dolls; she didn't know what she could give him. She wished she had another ha'penny for a sugar mouse.

And now it was time for Milly-next-door to put on her coat again and go home. Milly-Molly-Mandy and she said good-bye, and promised to write to each other and exchange paper dolls.

Milly-Molly-Mandy had never slept all alone before, and when bedtime came she felt quite pleased and excited. Mrs Hooker came and tucked her in, and she admired her new nightdress. Booby Rabbit was under the bedclothes, but he couldn't resist coming up

for a peep at Mrs Hooker, and Mrs Hooker
saw him and stroked his ears, and said she
would certainly have invited him if she had
thought he cared to come. And then she kissed
Milly-Molly-Mandy good-night, and Milly-
Molly-Mandy lay in the dark and enjoyed going
to sleep in a different bed.

Sunday was a nice day. They went to church
in the morning, and in the afternoon Milly-
Molly-Mandy painted paper dolls for little-
friend-Susan.

And then came Monday, and Milly-Molly-
Mandy's visit was over. It was in the afternoon
that Grandpa and Twinkletoes came with the
trap to fetch her home.

She was all ready but for slipping the sugar
mouse on to the mantelshelf with a note, 'With
Love from M. M. M.', where Mrs Hooker
would see it when she came in from seeing

Milly-Molly-Mandy off; and then Milly-Molly-Mandy was perched in her seat beside Grandpa.

And just as they drove off Mrs Hooker put a little packet of chocolate in Milly-Molly-Mandy's lap, to eat on the way home, and they cried 'Good-bye!' to each other, and waved, and soon Twinkletoes's twinkling feet had carried them right out of sight.

Presently Milly-Molly-Mandy, sitting in the trap, had yet another good idea; she could give the little packet of chocolate to Billy Blunt for a present!

So she said, 'Grandpa, would you be very disappointed if we didn't eat this chocolate?' adding in a whisper, 'I've got something in my bag for you!'

And Grandpa said, 'Milly-Molly-Mandy, I'm just feeling too excited to eat any chocolate now!'

So when they got home to the nice white cottage with the thatched roof, and Milly-Molly-Mandy had hugged Father and Mother and Grandpa and Grandma and Uncle and Aunty, she opened the leather bag, and gave:

Father a sugar mouse – and Father was pleased!

And Mother a handkerchief, marked 'M' for Mother. But when Mother saw it she said, 'Oh, how nice to have it all ready marked "M" for Mary!' And Milly-Molly-Mandy suddenly remembered Mother's real name was Mary, and she was only called Polly 'for short'! Milly-Molly-Mandy was so relieved that she had to jump up and down several times.

And then she gave Grandpa a sugar mouse – and Grandpa was pleased!

And Grandma the guards for her knitting-needles – and Grandma was pleased!

And Uncle a sugar mouse – and Uncle was pleased!

And Aunty a handkerchief marked 'A' for Aunty. But when Aunty saw it she said, 'How nice! Mine is marked too – "A" for Alice!' And Milly-Molly-Mandy suddenly remembered that Aunty and Alice both began with the same letter, and she was so very relieved that she had to jump up and down a great many times.

Next morning she ran down to the road to little-friend-Susan's and gave her the painted paper dolls, and little-friend-Susan was pleased!

And later in the day she saw Billy Blunt, and gave him the little packet of chocolate – and Billy Blunt was very surprised, and pleased too,

and he made her eat half, and it was the bigger half.

And then Milly-Molly-Mandy wrote a little letter to say 'thank you' to Mrs Hooker.

Milly-Molly-Mandy just does enjoy going away visiting!

Chapter Twelve

Milly-Molly-Mandy Gets to Know Teacher

Once upon a time there were changes at Milly-Molly-Mandy's school. Miss Sheppard, the head-mistress, was going away, and Miss Edwards, the second teacher, was to be head-mistress in her place, and live in the teacher's cottage just by the school, instead of coming in by the bus from the town each day.

Miss Edwards was very strict, and taught arithmetic and history and geography, and wore high collars.

Milly-Molly-Mandy wasn't particularly interested in the change, though she liked both Miss Sheppard and Miss Edwards quite well.

But one afternoon Miss Edwards gave her a
note to give to her Mother, and the note was
to ask if Milly-Molly-Mandy's Mother would be
so very good as to let Miss Edwards have a bed
at the nice white cottage with the thatched
roof for a night or two until Miss Edwards got
her new little house straight.

Father and Mother and Grandpa and
Grandma and Uncle and Aunty talked it over
during supper, and they thought they might
manage it for a few nights.

Milly-Molly-Mandy was very interested, and
tried to think what it would be like to have
Teacher sitting at supper with them, and going
to sleep in the spare room, as well as teaching
in school all day. And she couldn't help feeling
just a little bit glad that it was only to be for a
night or two.

Next day she took a note to school for

Teacher from Mother, to say, yes, they would be pleased to have her. And after school Milly-Molly-Mandy told little-friend-Susan and Billy Blunt about it.

And little-friend-Susan said, 'Oooh! Won't you have to behave properly! I'm glad she's not coming to us!'.

And Billy Blunt said, 'Huh! – hard lines!'

Milly-Molly-Mandy was quite glad Teacher was only coming to stay for a few nights.

Miss Edwards arrived at the nice white cottage with the thatched roof just before supper-time the following evening.

Milly-Molly-Mandy was looking out for her, and directly she heard the gate click she called Mother and ran and opened the front door wide, so that the hall lamp could shine down the path. And Teacher came in out of the dark, just as Mother hurried from the kitchen to welcome her.

Teacher thanked Mother very much for having her, and said she felt so dusty and untidy because she had been putting up shelves in her new little cottage ever since school was over.

So Mother said, 'Come right up to your room, Miss Edwards, and Milly-Molly-Mandy will bring you a jug of hot water. And then I expect you'll be glad of some supper straight away!'

So Milly-Molly-Mandy ran along to the kitchen for a jug of hot water, thinking how funny it was to hear Teacher's familiar voice away from school. She tapped very politely at the half-open door of the spare room (she could see Teacher tidying her hair in front of the dressing-table, by the candlelight), and

Teacher smiled at her as she took the steaming jug, and said:

'That's kind of you, Milly-Molly-Mandy! This is just what I want most. What a lovely smell of hot cakes!'

Milly-Molly-Mandy smiled back, though she was quite a bit surprised that Teacher should speak in that pleased, hungry sort of way – it was more the kind of way she, or little-friend-Susan, or Father or Mother or Grandpa or Grandma or Uncle or Aunty, might have spoken.

When Teacher came downstairs to the kitchen they all sat down to supper. Teacher's place was just opposite Milly-Molly-Mandy's, and every time she caught Milly-Molly-Mandy's eye she smiled across at her. And Milly-Molly-Mandy smiled back, and tried to remember to sit up, for she kept on almost expecting

Teacher to say, 'Head up, Milly-Molly-Mandy! Keep your elbows off the desk!' – but she never did!

They were all a little bit shy of Teacher, just at first; but soon Father and Mother and Grandpa and Grandma and Uncle and Aunty were talking away, and Teacher was talking too, and laughing. And she looked so different when she was laughing that Milly-Molly-Mandy found it quite difficult to get on with her bread-and-milk before it got cold. Teacher enjoyed the hot cakes, and wanted to know just how Mother made them. She asked a lot of questions, and Mother said she would teach Teacher how to do it, so that she could make them in her own new little kitchen.

Milly-Molly-Mandy thought how funny it would be for Teacher to start having lessons.

After supper Teacher asked Milly-Molly-

Mandy if she could make little sailor-girls, and when Milly-Molly-Mandy said no, Teacher drew a little sailor-girl, with a sailor-collar and sailor-hat and pleated skirt, on a folded piece of paper, and then she cut it out with Aunty's scissors. And when she unfolded the paper there was a whole row of little sailor-girls all holding hands.

Milly-Molly-Mandy did like it. She thought how funny it was that she should have known Teacher all that time and never known she could draw little sailor-girls.

Then Mother said, 'Now, Milly-Molly-Mandy, it is bedtime.' So Milly-Molly-Mandy kissed Father and Mother and Grandpa and Grandma and Uncle and Aunty, and went to shake hands with Teacher. But Teacher said she wanted a kiss too. So they kissed each other in quite a nice friendly way.

But still Milly-Molly-Mandy felt when she went upstairs she must get into bed extra quickly and quietly, because Teacher was in the house.

Next morning Milly-Molly-Mandy and Teacher went to school together. And as soon as they got there Teacher was just her usual self again, and told Milly-Molly-Mandy to sit up, or to get on with her work, as if she had never laughed at supper, or cut out little sailor-girls, or kissed anyone good-night.

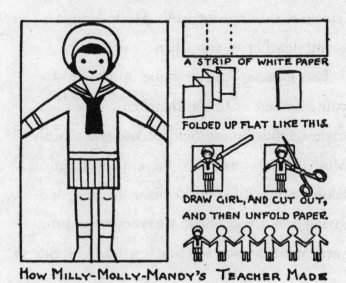

A STRIP OF WHITE PAPER

FOLDED UP FLAT LIKE THIS.

DRAW GIRL, AND CUT OUT, AND THEN UNFOLD PAPER.

HOW MILLY-MOLLY-MANDY'S TEACHER MADE LITTLE SAILOR-GIRLS.

After school Milly-Molly-Mandy showed little-friend-Susan and Billy Blunt the row of little sailor-girls.

And little-friend-Susan opened her eyes and said, 'Just fancy Teacher doing that!'

And Billy Blunt folded them up carefully in the creases so that he could see how they were made, and then he grinned and gave them back.

And little-friend-Susan and Billy Blunt didn't feel so very sorry for Milly-Molly-Mandy having Teacher to stay, then.

That evening Teacher came up to the nice white cottage with the thatched roof earlier than she did the day before. And when Milly-Molly-Mandy came into the kitchen from taking a nice meal out to Toby the dog, and giving him a good bedtime romp round the yard, what did she see but Teacher, with one of

Mother's big aprons on and her sleeves tucked up, learning how to make apple turn-overs for supper! And Mother was saying, 'Always mix pastry with a light hand,' and Teacher was looking so interested, and didn't seem in the least to know she had a streak of flour down one cheek.

When Teacher saw Milly-Molly-Mandy she said, 'Come along, Milly-Molly-Mandy, and have a cooking-lesson with me, it's such fun!'

So Milly-Molly-Mandy's Mother gave her a little piece of dough, and she stood by Teacher's side, rolling it out and making it into a ball again; but she was much more interested in watching Teacher being taught. And Teacher did everything she was told, and tried so hard that her cheeks got quite pink.

When the turn-overs were all made there was a small piece of dough left on the board, so Teacher shaped it into the most beautiful little bird; and the bird and the turn-overs were all popped into the oven, together with Milly-Molly-Mandy's piece (which had been a pig and a cat and a teapot, but ended up a little grey loaf).

When Father and Mother and Grandpa and Grandma and Uncle and Aunty and Teacher and Milly-Molly-Mandy sat down to supper, Teacher put her finger on her lips to Milly-Molly-Mandy when the apple turn-overs came on, so that Milly-Molly-Mandy shouldn't tell who made them until they had been tasted. And Teacher watched anxiously, and presently Mother said, 'How do you like these turn-overs?' And everybody said they were most delicious, and then Milly-Molly-Mandy couldn't wait any longer, and she called out, 'Teacher made them!' and everybody was so surprised.

What did she see but Teacher learning how to make apple turn-overs

Milly-Molly-Mandy didn't eat the little grey-brown loaf, because she didn't quite fancy it (Toby the dog did, though), and she felt she couldn't eat the little golden-brown bird, because it really looked too good to be eaten just yet. So she took it to school with her next day, to share with little-friend-Susan and Billy Blunt.

And little-friend-Susan said, 'Isn't it pretty? Isn't Teacher clever?'

And Billy Blunt said, 'Fancy Teacher playing with dough!'

And little-friend-Susan and Billy Blunt didn't feel at all sorry for Milly-Molly-Mandy having Teacher to stay, then.

The next day was Saturday, and Teacher's furniture had come, and she was busy all day arranging it and getting the curtains and the pictures up. And Milly-Molly-Mandy with little-

friend-Susan and Billy Blunt came in the
afternoon to help. And they ran up and down
stairs, and fetched hammers and nails, and held
things, and made themselves very useful indeed.

And at four o'clock Teacher sent Billy Blunt
out to get some cakes from Mrs Hubble's shop,
while the others laid the table in the pretty

little sitting-room. And they had a nice kind of
picnic, with Milly-Molly-Mandy and little-
friend-Susan sharing a cup, and Billy Blunt

having a saucer for a plate, because everything wasn't unpacked yet. And they all laughed and talked, and were as happy as anything.

And when Teacher said it was time to send them all off home Milly-Molly-Mandy was so sorry to think Teacher wasn't coming to sleep in the spare room any more that she wanted to kiss Teacher without being asked. And she actually did it, too. And little-friend-Susan and Billy Blunt didn't look a bit surprised, either.

And after that, somehow, it didn't seem to matter that Teacher was strict in school, for they knew that she was really just a very nice, usual sort of person inside all the time!

Chapter Thirteen

Milly-Molly-Mandy Goes to a *Fête*

Once upon a time, while Milly-Molly-Mandy was shopping in the village for Mother, she saw a poster on a board outside Mr Blunt's corn-shop. So she stopped to read it, and she found that there was to be a *fête* held in the playing-field, with sports and competitions for children, and other things for grown-ups. And while she was reading Billy Blunt looked out of the shop door.

Milly-Molly-Mandy said, 'Hullo, Billy!'

And Billy Blunt grinned and said, 'Hullo, Milly-Molly-Mandy!' and he came and looked at the poster too.

'When's the *fête* to be?' said Milly-Molly-Mandy, and Billy Blunt pointed with his toe to the date. And then he pointed to the words, 'Hundred-yard races, three-legged races etc.,' and said, 'I'm going in for them.'

'Are you?' said Milly-Molly-Mandy, and began to be interested. She thought a *fête* would be quite fun, and decided to ask Mother when she got home if she might go to it too.

A day or two later, as Milly-Molly-Mandy was swinging on the meadow-gate after school, she saw someone running along in the middle of the road in a very steady, businesslike fashion. And who should it be but Billy Blunt?

'Hullo, Billy! Where're you going?' said Milly-Molly-Mandy.

Billy Blunt slowed up and wiped his forehead, panting. 'I'm getting into training,' said Billy Blunt, 'for the races.'

Milly-Molly-Mandy thought that was a very good idea.

'I'm going to do some running every day,' said Billy Blunt, 'till the *fête*.'

Milly-Molly-Mandy was sure Billy Blunt would win.

And then Billy Blunt asked if Milly-Molly-Mandy could count minutes, because it would be nice to have someone to time his running sometimes. Milly-Molly-Mandy couldn't, because she had never tried. But after that she practised counting minutes with the kitchen clock, till she got to know just about how fast to count sixty so that it was almost exactly a minute.

And the next day Billy Blunt stood right at one end of the meadow, by the nice white cottage with the thatched roof where Milly-Molly-Mandy lived, and Milly-Molly-Mandy stood at the other end. And when Billy Blunt shouted 'Go!' and began running, Milly-Molly-Mandy shut her eyes tight so that she wouldn't think of anything else, and began counting steadily. And Billy Blunt reached her side in just over a minute and a half. They did it several times, but Billy Blunt couldn't manage to do it in less time.

After that they tied their ankles together – Billy Blunt's left and Milly-Molly-Mandy's right – with Billy Blunt's scarf, and practised running with three legs across the field. It was such fun, and Milly-Molly-Mandy shouted with laughter sometimes because they just couldn't help falling over. But Billy Blunt was rather solemn, and very keen to do it properly – though even he couldn't keep from letting out a laugh now and then, when they got very entangled.

By the time of the *fête* Billy Blunt was able
to get across the meadow in a little over a
minute, and their three-legged running was
really quite good, so they were full of hopes
for winning some prizes in the sports.

The day of the *fête* was nice and fine, even if
not very warm. But, as Billy Blunt said, it was
just as well to have it a bit cool for the sports.
As it was Bank Holiday nearly everybody in the
village turned up, paying their sixpences at the
gate, and admiring the flags, and saying 'Hullo!'
or 'How do you do?' to each other.

Milly-Molly-Mandy went with her Father and
Mother and Grandpa and Grandma and Uncle
and Aunty. And little-friend-Susan was there
with her mother, who was also looking after
Miss Muggins's niece Jilly, as Miss Muggins
didn't care much for *fêtes*. And Mr Jakes, the
Postman, was there with his wife; and Mr

Off they all started

Rudge, the Blacksmith, in his Sunday suit.

There were coconut-shies (Uncle won a coconut); and throwing little hoops (three throws a penny) over things spread out on a table (Mother got a pocket-comb, but she tried to get an alarm-clock), and lots of other fun.

And then the Children's Sports began. Milly-Molly-Mandy paid a penny for a try at walking along a very narrow board to reach a red balloon at the other end, but she toppled off before she got it, and everybody laughed. (Miss Muggins's Jilly got a balloon.)

Then they entered for the three-legged race – little-friend-Susan and Miss Muggins's Jilly together, and Milly-Molly-Mandy and Billy Blunt (because they had practised), and a whole row of other boys and girls.

A man tied their ankles, and shouted 'Go!' and off they all started, and everybody laughed, and couples kept stumbling and tumbling round, but Milly-Molly-Mandy and Billy Blunt careered steadily along till they reached the winning-post!

Then everybody laughed and clapped like anything, and Billy Blunt pulled the string from round their ankles in a great hurry and cleared off, and Milly-Molly-Mandy had to take his box of chocolates for him, as well as her own.

Then there was the hundred yards race for boys. There was one rather shabbily dressed boy who had stood looking on at all the games, so Father asked him if he didn't want to join in, and he said he hadn't any money. So Father paid for him to join in the race, and he looked so pleased!

A man shouted 'Go!' and off went all the boys in a mass – and how they did run! Milly-Molly-Mandy was so excited that she had to keep jumping up and down. But Billy Blunt presently got a little bit ahead of the others. (Milly-Molly-Mandy held herself tight.) And then he got a little bit farther – and so did the shabby boy – only not so far as Billy Blunt. And then Billy Blunt saw him out of the corner of his eye as he ran, and then the race was over, and somehow the shabby boy had won. And he got a striped tin of toffee.

And Billy Blunt grinned at the shabby boy, who looked so happy hugging his tin of toffee, and asked him his name, and where he lived, and would he come and practise racing with him in the meadow next Saturday.

The next day, as Milly-Molly-Mandy and Billy Blunt and one or two others were coming home from school, they saw a big man with a suitcase waiting at the crossroads for the bus, which went every hour into the town. And just as the bus came in sight the man's hat blew off away down the road, ever such a distance. The man looked for a moment as if he didn't know what to do; and then he caught sight of them and shouted:

'Hi! – can any of you youngsters run?'

Milly-Molly-Mandy said, 'Billy Blunt can!' And instantly off went Billy Blunt down the road in his best racing style. And just as the bus pulled up at the stopping-place, he picked up the hat and came tearing back with it.

'I should just say you can run!' said the man.
'You've saved me an hour's wait for the next
bus, and a whole lot of business besides.'

'What a good thing you were in training!'
said Milly-Molly-Mandy to Billy Blunt, as the
bus went off.

'Huh! more sense, that, than just racing,' said
Billy Blunt, putting his hair straight.

The furry bundle has arrived.

'Okay, okay. So hang me. I killed a bird. For pity's sake, I'm a cat.'

Get your claws out for the hilarious antics of Tuffy and his family as told by the killer cat himself. If you know cats, you'll understand.

'infectiously funny and highly readable'
– Independent

ANNE FINE
The Return of the
Killer Cat

ANNE FINE
The Diary of a
Killer Cat

Cover illustrations © Steve Cox

'A brilliant tale of catastrophe and pussy pandemonium'
– *Daily Telegraph*

young puffin modern classics
THE VERY BEST STORIES FOR CHILDREN

great books
for you to enjoy

Wonderful stories for
each new generation

puffin.co.uk